Abracadabra!

WHOA!
Amusement Park Gone Wild!

Anything can happen when you wave your magic wand!

Join the Abracadabra Club in all their Magical Mysteries.

#1: **POOF!** Rabbits Everywhere!

#2: **Boo!** Ghosts in the School!

#3: **PRESTO!** Magic Treasure!

#4: **YEEPS!** Secret in the Statue!

#5: **ZAP!** Science Fair Surprise!

#6: **YIKES!** It's Alive!

#7: **WHOA!** Amusement Park Gone Wild!

Abracadabra!

WHOA!
Amusement Park Gone Wild!

By Peter Lerangis
Illustrated by Jim Talbot

A
LITTLE APPLE
PAPERBACK

SCHOLASTIC INC.
New York   Toronto   London   Auckland   Sydney
Mexico City   New Delhi   Hong Kong   Buenos Aires

*Dedicated to the memory of Nunley's Carousel,
Baldwin, N.Y.*

ISBN 0-439-38938-0

12 11 10 9 8 7 6 5 4 3 2 1   3 4 5 6 7 8/0
                                              40

Printed in the U.S.A.
First printing, April 2003

Contents

1

Poob Lick No Tickee

"I want a big Crump's burger, with Ferris wheel fries and a milkshake!" shouted Jessica Frimmel as she raced out of the family car.

Quincy Norton rushed after her, nearly losing his glasses, which always hung crooked on his face. "I want to beat the high score on the Cyber Skill pinball machine!" he announced. "I need one hundred ten thousand two hundred thirteen points."

"I want to kick Filbert!" squealed Noah Frimmel, Jessica's little brother.

Noah was six and a half years old, and he liked to kick things. Sometimes he kicked Jessica and got into big trouble. But when he went to Crump's Playworld, he kicked Filbert the merry-go-round horse, which wasn't so bad. Filbert was big and shiny, with a crack in his ear and dents in his sides. Kids had been kicking Filbert and the other horses for seventy-five years — ever since Crump's Playworld opened. It was a tradition.

Crump's was famous all over New England. The merry-go-round was in a glass building, which was big enough to fit pinball games, photo booths, air hockey and Foosball tables, shooting galleries, and a coin-stamping machine. Next to the building was Crump's fast-food Playworld Grill. Outside was a kiddie boat ride, go-carts, miniature golf, a small roller coaster, a Tilt-A-Whirl, and a rocket ride. The Ferris wheel broke down a lot, and some of the games hadn't worked for months. But it didn't really matter. Kids still loved Crump's.

If you asked Jessica, she'd say that Crump's was the Second Best Reason for Living in Rebus, Massachusetts.

The First Best Reason, she'd claim, was the Abracadabra Club. "Abracadabra" stood for "Amazing Better-Rebus-Area Company of Amateur Detectives and Baffling Real-magic Artists." (Quincy thought of that name. He was the smartest kid in fourth grade.) The Abracadabra Club was the only club for magicians *and* detectives at Rebus Elementary School. Jessica was the leader, or Main Brain.

Besides Jessica and Quincy, the club's other main members were Selena Cruz and

Max Bleeker. All four were going to spend the day at Crump's. Today, they had free passes to all rides. That's because the club had performed a magic show for Crump's at its seventy-fifth birthday celebration.

Jessica ran up the path to the Playworld Grill. Selena and Max were already there, staring at a sign in the window:

```
┌─────────────────────────────────────┐
│           PUBLIC NOTICE              │
│    RESTAURANT CLOSED FOR REPAIRS     │
└─────────────────────────────────────┘
```

"Poob . . . lick . . . no . . . tickee?" said Noah, trying to read the sign.

"That means it's closed," said Mr. Frimmel, Noah and Jessica's dad.

"Stand back!" shouted Max, whooshing his big black cape. "I shall cast a magic spell to open the clocks!"

"*Locks,*" Jessica corrected him.

Max wore a cape and a top hat every day, even to school. He also mixed up his words when he was nervous. He really, truly believed he was a wizard. His spells never worked, but that didn't stop Max.

"ABRACADABRA . . . ZIP . . . TUM-BLO!" Max chanted. "Or wait. Is it TIM-BLO . . . ?"

"We must figure out why the grill is closed!" Quincy declared, taking a notepad out of his backpack. Quincy loved mysteries almost as much as he loved magic. "Any clues?"

"We can just ask," said Selena.

"Good suggestion!" Quincy jotted it down on his pad.

From the carousel entrance, a voice shouted, "Hey, what are you waiting around for? Can't you read?"

It was Charlene Crump, the grand-daughter of Elwood and Fiona Crump, who owned the park. Charlene was in fourth grade at Rebus Elementary School. Her hair was like a volcano of brown curls. They tumbled over her eyes and landed in a heap on her shoulders.

"I can read!" said Noah proudly, pointing at the sign. "Poob lick no tickee!"

"Charlene, how come the grill is closed?" asked Jessica's mom, Mrs. Frimmel.

Charlene shrugged. "The same reason the Ferris wheel is closed. And the Foosball table and the coin-stamping machine are broken. Everything's old. It costs too much to repair things. And we don't make enough money."

"But Crump's is famous!" Selena said. "Everyone comes here!"

"Not as many people as in the old days,"

Charlene explained. "We used to be open seven days a week. Now we're open only Thursday through Sunday. Business stinks. And it's only going to get worse. Grandpa says there's going to be a new historic site, Old Brattle Village, right next to Rebus. Soon everyone's going to want to go there. It will take business away from us. If Crump's can't pass the inspection next week, Grandpa's going to sell the place. Which is fine with me. They'll tear it down. They'll make it into a gas station or something. And I won't have to come in on weekends to help out anymore!"

"But Crump's is the coolest!" Max said. "If *my* grandparents owned it, I would help out on the weekdays, too!"

Charlene groaned. "I never come here besides the weekends. *Ever!*"

As Charlene bounced away, Jessica's heart beat fast. Crump's — a pile of broken metal and wood? Filbert, smashed into splinters?

A gas station?

"She must be joking," Selena said.

"Charlene doesn't joke," Quincy replied.

Jessica stepped into the carousel building and looked around. The floor was all scuffed and scraped. The horses were chipped and fading. Yellow tape covered the broken machines. Jessica looked around for Mr. Crump, whom everyone called Grandpa. He was sitting in the ticket booth outside, reading a newspaper. No one was waiting in line.

Jessica's dad let out a long, low whistle. "Man, this place will never pass inspection."

"We have to *do* something!" Jessica exclaimed. "We have to save Crump's."

"I say we take our free rides while we have the chance," Max said, waving his passes in the air.

"I'm hungry!" Noah whined. "I want to eat now!"

"Let's go to Frankie Fry's for lunch," said Mrs. Frimmel, "then come back for rides, and *then* save Crump's."

Everyone agreed.

Frankie Fry's Franks 'n' Fries was on the other side of town, near Rebus Elementary School. It was shaped like a big green bucket, with giant fake fries sticking out of the roof. Next to the restaurant was Frankie's Funland, a playground made of tubes that looked like hot dogs.

In front stood a statue of the Frankie Fry's mascot, Mr. Spuds. He was a clown with curly brown hair and a long nose like a french fry. Today he held a sign that said, FRANKIE FRY'S FRANKS 'N' FRIES — THE FASTEST GROWING FOOD CHAIN IN NEW EN-

GLAND. WATCH FOR ANOTHER FUNLAND OPENING IN YOUR NEIGHBORHOOD!

The Abracadabra Club quickly ordered meals and sat down together. Jessica's parents sat with Noah, who ate his meal in about twenty seconds and then vanished into Funland.

"Okay, Crump's *has* to pass inspection," Jessica said. "What can we do?"

"Hypnotize the inspectors?" Max suggested.

"We could make the walls beautiful," said Selena, "by painting a mural. Well, *I* could do it, because I'm good in art. The rest of you could mop, scrub, and fix things."

"My dad can repair machines," Max said. "The Ferris wheel is a machine."

"He can't repair *everything*," remarked Selena. "It would take a whole village to fix up a place as broken down as Crump's."

"A whole village . . ." Quincy began to write in his notepad. "Excellent idea, Selena!"

"It is?" Selena asked.

"We'll let all of Rebus know," Quincy continued. "We'll get everyone to help. We can call it the 'Big Cleanup at Crump's.' We can put flyers all over town."

Jessica jumped up. "And we'll have entertainment — and music. I'll ask Professor Platt. He's the leader of the Rebus Community Band, and he lives in my neighborhood. Plus, he's best friends with Mayor Kugel. Maybe the mayor will come, too!"

"Mr. Beamish can call the TV station and newspapers!" Selena said. Mr. Beamish was the supervisor of the Abracadabra Club. He was also Jessica, Selena, and Quincy's teacher.

Quincy was writing so fast he didn't notice his glasses slipping. "I'll make a sign-up sheet. We can put it up tomorrow."

"Perfect!" Jessica said, digging into her cheese fries. "SAVE CRUMP'S!"

"SAVE CRUMP'S!" shouted Max.

"Oops," said Quincy as his glasses fell to the table.

Selena brushed her hair, smiling dreamily. "I've always wanted to be on TV."

2

Shazammed

"SIGN UP NOW!" shouted Quincy, walking up and down the Rebus Elementary School lobby the next morning.

"HELP US SAVE CRUMP'S!" Jessica called out. She, Max, and Selena stood beside a card table borrowed from the principal, Mr. McElroy. As kids walked by, the Abracadabra Club handed out flyers.

"Excuse me," said Andrew Flingus.

14

```
**SAVE CRUMP'S PLAYWORLD

FROM ~~DISTR~~ DESTRUCTION!!**
BIG CLEANUP DAY AT CRUMP'S!!!
THIS SATURDAY ONLY!
BRING YOUR WHOLE FAMILY!!!


BROUGHT TO YOU BY THE WORLD-FAMOUS

ABRACADABRA CLUB

                          Jessica Frimmel, Main Brain
```

Andrew was the most awful boy in the fourth grade. He took a flyer and then blew his nose in it.

Selena nearly turned green with horror. "Ewww!"

"BE GONE," shouted Max, waving his magic wand, "OR I SHALL CHANGE YOU INTO A TOE!"

"He means *toad*," Jessica said.

"Ribbit, ribbit!" croaked Andrew, hopping away. He disappeared into another crowd, at the other end of the hall. It was a much bigger crowd than the one gathered around the Abracadabra Club. They were all holding flyers, too.

"COME ONE, COME ALL!" shouted the voice of Doug Jones. Everyone called Doug "Bug" because he was so annoying.

"Brrrrrup!" burped the burp of Andrew Flingus.

Max tapped the shoulder of Bruce Minsky, who was in the back of the crowd. "Are Bug and Andrew signing people up for the Big Cleanup, too?"

Bruce gave Max the flyer he was holding. Jessica leaned over his shoulder and read:

> **HEY, KIDS!!**
>
> **IT'S BRAND-NEW—**
>
> **COME SEE THE <u>NUMBER 1</u>**
>
> **MAGIC CLUB IN ALL OF REBUS:**
>
> # *THE SHAZAM CLUB!*
>
> AFTER SCHOOL TODAY IN THE GYM

"The Shazam Club?" Jessica said.

"How dare they," Selena grumbled. She took out her hairbrush and ran it through her hair. Selena always brushed her hair when she was angry. Also when she was happy, or nervous, or confused, or bored, or excited. "*We're* the number-one magic club. The first and the best."

"They're stealing our idea!" Max declared.

Jessica took the Shazam Club's flyer and marched across the lobby. In the middle of the crowd stood Bug and Andrew. Bug was wearing a fancy top hat, twice as big as Max's. He wore a black suit and a fake mustache, too.

The nerve of him. Jessica would never forget the time Bug tried to join the Abracadabra Club. His tricks were awful. He had almost ruined the club's seventy-fifth birthday show at Crump's.

Jessica barged in front of the line. "Bug Jones, why are you copying us?"

Bug twirled his fake mustache. "Copy? Did the great Houdini copy Magical Marvin?"

"Who was Magical Marvin?" Jessica asked.

"See? No one ever heard of him!" Bug

replied. "Like no one will remember the Abracadabra Club! Oops, what's this behind your ear?"

Bug reached behind Jessica's left ear and pulled out a quarter.

"Cool!" someone in the crowd shouted.

"That is the dumbest trick in the world," Jessica said. "You had the coin in your hand all along. I'll show you a *real* trick."

Jessica grabbed Bug's quarter with her right hand. She held up her left arm, keeping her elbow bent. Then she started rubbing the coin into the back of her arm, just above the elbow. "If I rub hard enough, it will disappear!"

Suddenly, the quarter fell to the floor.

"HAR! HAR! HAR!" Andrew laughed. "Some trick!"

Jessica quickly picked it up. "If at first you don't succeed, try, try again!"

This time she rubbed it even harder. Then she held up her right hand — and it was empty. The quarter had disappeared.

She smiled and looked up at the crowd, but Bug was blocking her. No one had seen the trick! "Come see the famous Shazam Club!" Bug shouted.

"Bug Jones, that's not fair!" Jessica protested.

Andrew leaned over and burped in Jessica's ear. "Hey, no one ever said the Abracadabra Club was the only game in town."

That afternoon, in a small room in the Rebus Elementary School basement, Jessica tapped her magic wand on a desk. "We have to stop them!"

School was over. The Abracadabra Club had gathered for its Monday meeting. It met every Monday and Thursday in its own basement club room. Because Jessica was the club's Main Brain, she ran the meetings.

"You're supposed to say, 'I call this meeting to order,'" said Quincy, opening the official Abracadabra Club Journal. He was the club's Scribe, which meant "Writer." In the Journal, he kept notes about each meeting. In the Abracadabra Files, he listed the club's magic tricks (and how to do them). During each mystery, he kept a Clues Book. And when the mystery was solved, he wrote about it in the Mystery Log. Quincy wrote all the time — even while he was eating and walking. Some said he wrote while he was sleeping, too. But nobody could prove that.

"OK — let's have some order!" Jessica barked.

"Order?" The door swung open, and Mr. Beamish came in. "I'll have a turkey sandwich!"

Although Mr. Beamish was a teacher during the week, on weekends, he became Stanley Beamish, Semi-famous Wild West Magician. He performed his own magic shows at parties. With his shiny bald head and pointy beard, he looked like a large gnome or a very friendly wizard.

"Mr. Beamish, we *must* talk about the Shazam Club," Selena said, brushing her hair. "Their magic stinks. But their costumes are beautiful, and they make us look bad." Selena was the Club Designer, in charge of the club's costumes, scenery, and props.

"Well, they have a right to do magic, too," said Mr. Beamish, sitting at his desk. "We must prove ourselves to be the better club, that's all."

"HA!" said Max, who was the club Numa. No one knew for sure what that meant, but somehow it fit Max. "We're the

Abracadabra Club! We're the best! We're the original! We're —"

A blast of music sounded from above them. A loud cheer rang out.

Jessica ran out of the club room and into the basement. The others followed her up the stairs and through the hallways, all the way to the gym.

The doors were open. A big banner over the entrance said WELCOME TO THE SHAZAM CLUB! Kids were crowding into the gym. Dozens of them.

"We're toast," said Selena.

3

The Big Cleanup

BLAAAAT! HONNNK! SCREEEK!

"Please, trumpets, not so loud!" shouted Professor Platt.

The Rebus Community Band sounded like a barnyard on a bad day. But it didn't matter. The Abracadabra Club's hard work had paid off. It was Saturday, and Crump's Playworld was full of helpers. The Big

Cleanup was about to begin. People were in work clothes, carrying paintbrushes and hammers and brooms and water buckets. Mr. Spuds, the Frankie Fry's clown, was passing out free hot dogs. Even the mayor was there. Jessica couldn't help grinning.

"Look at that mob," said Max, staring at the crowd. "All of Rebus is here! Half of Massachusetts! They're screaming . . . for MAX THE MAGNIFICENT!"

"One hundred and forty-seven people are here," said Quincy, writing in his notepad. "One hundred and fifty-nine, if you count the babies in strollers."

"Those inspectors will give this place an A-plus!" Jessica exclaimed as she set up the Abracadabra Club table near the mayor's platform.

"Ready for some magic, Mayor Kugel?" Max asked.

The mayor laughed. "Maybe you can cast a spell to tune up the band."

Selena began pulling the table away from the platform. "We can't set ourselves up *here*. We have to be near the Ferris wheel. It's a perfect background for our TV and newspaper photo ops. Now, where should we put our Abracadabra Club banner?"

They walked right by Charlene Crump, who was holding a huge ring of keys. "In the garbage," she grumbled.

"What are you so grumpy about?" asked Jessica.

"My grandpa just had the Foosball table and coin-stamping machine fixed," Charlene said. "That means more work for me. I'm the one who has to unlock all the power boxes. Whose idea was this stupid cleanup, anyway?"

Behind Charlene, people were working

hard on the carousel building. One team was cleaning the glass walls. Another team was sweeping the floor. A few people were painting things and shining the faded brass poles of the carousel.

"This is fun, Charlene," Jessica said. "Besides, you're not working half as hard as everyone else."

Mayor Kugel stepped onto the platform and held the mike. "WELCOME, MY FELLOW CITIZENS OF FAIR REBUS," he said. "TODAY, WE GATHER TO HELP OUR FRIENDS AND NEIGHBORS, MR. AND MRS. ELWOOD CRUMP!"

"My grandfather doesn't like him," Charlene said. "But I do. Two years ago, he said this place was an eyesore. He tried to close it down. Maybe someday he will!"

As Charlene walked away, Selena made a face. "Once a grouch, always a grouch . . ."

She spotted a long metal bar, sticking through two hooks on the Ferris wheel's power box. She figured the bar was there to keep the box shut. It would make a perfect hook for the Abracadabra Club banner.

BLEEEET! RAAAAACK! WHOMMMP! went the Rebus band. Mr. Spuds put his hands over his ears. So did a lot of other people.

A TV van pulled up to the curb. It was labeled with a WRBS logo. A man with a microphone climbed out, followed by a woman holding a TV camera.

Selena began brushing her hair furiously. "Smile! This is our big break!"

But another van had parked, too. This one had a different sign — JONES CONSTRUCTION. Its side door slid open. Bug, Andrew, Bruce Minsky, and two other kids stumbled out. They were dressed in white shirts and shiny

black pants, with top hats and black velvet capes. Bug was holding a cordless microphone. "LADIES AND GENTLEMEN, WHAT YOU'VE ALL BEEN WAITING FOR!"

Mr. Jones, Bug's dad, tossed something to the ground. A cloud of smoke whooshed up. When it cleared, the kids were gone.

They reappeared in front of the merry-go-round, with their backs to the crowd. Across their capes, spelled out in silver paint were the words SHAZAM CLUB.

Music blared from the van. A voice sang: *"The Shazam Club is here, let's give them a cheer!"* to a rock beat.

The TV crew gathered around. As two cameras focused on the Shazam Club, Andrew began drooling and making monster faces.

"Theme music?" Jessica said.

"Smoke?" Quincy added.

"And look at those beautiful capes," Selena muttered softly.

"A real magic club is *not* about fancy costumes and effects that your *parents* bought for you!" Jessica snapped.

"I'm getting out of here," muttered Charlene.

"PAY NO ATTENTION TO THOSE KIDS BEHIND THE FANCY CAPES!" Max called out. "MAX THE MAGNIFICENT AND THE ABRACADABRA CLUB ARE HERE!"

But no one was listening to Max. With a loud *poof*, another flash of smoke went up. When it cleared, the merry-go-round was running — and all of the Shazam Club members were on horses.

People in the crowd "oooohed" and

"aaaahed." Mr. Spuds jumped on a horse backward and fell off. The TV cameras caught every moment.

"This is the dumbest thing I've ever seen," Max declared.

"There goes my television debut," Selena grumbled.

"We have to get the crowd's attention," Jessica said. She took a long rope from the magic table and tied a knot in it. Then she held up a pair of scissors. *"I need a volunteer from the audience!"*

Noah, who had just arrived with his and Jessica's mom, ran forward. Jessica gave him the scissors and told him to cut the rope right near the knot.

Noah sliced the rope, bowed eleven times, and ran back to his mother.

Jessica held up the rope for all to see. "Now I have two smaller ropes with a knot in the middle. I shall wrap them around my hand. The knot will magically disappear — and one long rope will remain. But only if you say Abracadabra on the count of three!"

Jessica's trick was working. One by one, the people in the crowd were turning to watch. Even the TV crew was coming over! As Jessica wrapped the rope, Max, Selena, and Quincy chanted together: "One . . . two . . . three . . ."

"SHAZAM!" shouted Bug Jones through a microphone.

Jessica stood, waiting. But Bug had startled the crowd. Everyone turned toward the Shazam Club. So did the TV crew.

Bug was near the merry-go-round, looking nervously off to his left. "I said, SHAZAM!"

Andrew came running from the bathroom. "Uh, here I am!" He took off his top hat, reached in, and pulled out a fake bunny rabbit, all white but covered with chocolate stains.

As the crowd clapped, Andrew made the bunny take a bow. The cameras came in for a close-up.

"We're losing them again!" said Jessica. Then she called out, "Um, ahem . . . *will someone please say Abracadabra?*"

"Let's move closer to the media," said Selena, pulling the table over toward the Shazam Club.

"UM . . . NEXT I SHALL DO A LASSO TRICK!" Bug took out a long, heavy rope and spun it. It flew out of his hands.

"Uh, we did that on purpose — HAR! HAR! HAR!" laughed Andrew, as Bug went running after the rope. "And now I will pull paper clips out of my nose!"

Selena quickly stepped in front of Andrew and smiled into the camera. "Ladies and gentlemen, Jessica will finish her amazing trick if you say Abracadabra!"

The crowd finally paid attention. "ABRACADABRA!" a few people yelled.

Jessica unwrapped the rope — *one* rope, with no knot! The crowd let out a nice, loud cheer. "Remarkable!" shouted Mayor Kugel.

Then Bug came running back. He was carrying one end of the lasso. The other end trailed behind him. "Wait!" he shouted. "I shall now wrap *my* rope around this special magic wand — and, um, make the wand disappear!"

Bug pulled a metal pole out of his belt. He wrapped and wrapped the rope around it. But about halfway down the pole, the rope pulled tight. The other end was still stuck somewhere near the boat ride. "Oops," Bug said.

"MY, MY — I SHOULD HELP THAT POOR YOUNG MAN!" Max shouted,

pulling a red handkerchief out of his cape. "BUT ALL I HAVE IS THIS ONE SMALL HANDKERCHIEF. HMMM... HOW ABOUT A MAGIC SPELL — ABRACADABRA... FLEET... NUMISMO!"

Max gave the red handkerchief a tug. Suddenly, he was pulling a whole string of handkerchiefs from his cape!

CRRRAAASSHHHH!

The coin-stamping machine suddenly fell open — dumping hundreds of blank coins on the ground!

The crowd began talking and pointing, looking past the Abracadabra Club.

"Yeeps!" said Quincy.

Max slapped his forehead. "Uh-oh, I chanted the coin-appearing spell by mistake. The handkerchief spell is ABRACADABRA . . . FLOOT . . . NOMISMOO!"

CRRRREEEEAAK!

The broken Ferris wheel slowly started turning, all by itself. "Look!" someone shouted. "It's haunted!"

"*Max, stop chanting!*" Selena shouted.

"Did I do *that*?" Max said.

Grandpa Crump raced over to the Ferris wheel. But halfway there, his feet began splashing in water.

FLLOOOOSH!

Water came flooding out of the boat ride. It gushed over the ground, toward the crowd. Selena slid on the soles of her fancy leather shoes. She grabbed on to Quincy. He fell over, too. Half the crowd was laughing. The other half was trying to leave, to keep from getting wet.

The TV cameras were recording it all.

Jessica's heart sank. Crump's was falling apart, right before their eyes.

.

4

Crump's in the Dumps?

That night, the Abracadabra Club gathered at Jessica's house to watch the local news. A few neighbors were over, too, including Professor Platt. About halfway through the program, the TV announcer said, "It started as a beautiful day at Crump's Playworld — a day of fun, hard work . . . and magic tricks!"

Max jumped up. "This is us!"

"I was on a TV commercial once!" said Noah.

"SSHHHH!" said Jessica.

The TV screen filled up with the Shazam Club banner. In the background, the Shazam Club's theme music played. Then, after a big puff of smoke, Andrew was pulling a fake rabbit out of a hat. The crowd was cheering like crazy. "But these talented young magicians never had a chance," the announcer went on, "among the creaky rides and broken dreams that are Crump's Playworld."

Jessica and Quincy were on the screen now, falling into the water. Max was waving his wand, looking confused. Selena was screaming and taking her shoes off.

Watching herself, Selena made a sad face. "Those shoes cost a fortune," she explained.

Then the camera showed Grandpa

Crump trying to fix the Ferris wheel, with water gushing under his feet. The announcer's voice became very serious. "With all the old amusement park's troubles, and historic Old Brattle Village soon to open, the next big machine that swings over Crump's may not be a Ferris wheel . . . but instead, a wrecking ball."

"WAAAAH!" cried Noah, stomping out of the TV room.

"There goes the inspection," Quincy said.

"So sad," said Professor Platt.

Jessica's heart sank. Crump's was doomed, unless the Abracadabra Club could do something. "Let's go out to the garage, guys," she said. "We need a plan."

Jessica, Max, Quincy, and Selena went outside. It was a warm night, and the garage smelled of motor oil and grass clippings.

Selena groaned. "We looked *so* stupid on the news."

"And Bug and Andrew looked so good," Quincy added.

"The TV didn't even show *one* of our tricks," Max complained.

"Guys, how can you even *think* about us?" Jessica blurted out. "What about Crump's? We were supposed to *save* it — and look what happened!"

"It's my fault." Max's eyes were misty. "That handkerchief spell always gives me trouble."

"It's not your fault, Max," Selena said. "It's none of our faults. Crump's is old and run down."

"But the coin-stamping machine had just been fixed," Jessica said. "*It* wasn't run down. But it broke, too!"

Quincy began writing in his notepad.

"Coin-stamping machine . . . Ferris wheel . . . boat ride. Three things. Does it seem odd they would break at the same time — while a TV crew was watching?"

"Maybe someone did it on purpose," Selena said. "Someone who doesn't like Crump's!"

"Everybody likes Crump's," said Jessica.

"Why would someone want to destroy it?" Quincy asked. "What's the motive?"

"Someone who thought it was really, really ugly?" Selena said.

Quincy began writing furiously. "You mean . . . an eyesore."

"Right," said Selena.

"That's it . . . yes, you've got it, Selena!" Quincy was so excited, he nearly dropped his glasses. "Remember what Charlene said? Two years ago the mayor wanted to close Crump's. He thought it was an eyesore!"

"Mayor Kugel?" Selena shook her head. "But he couldn't have broken anything. He was on the platform the whole time."

"He could have had helpers do it for him, sneaking around while the magic shows were on!" Quincy said. "First of all, no one would suspect him. And with the cameras there, the whole TV audience could see how run down Crump's was. He'd prove to everyone that it should be destroyed!"

"You guys — he's our *mayor*," said Selena. "He's done great things for Rebus. Half the town is named for him. Kugel Park. Kugel Tower. The Kugel Center for the Performing Arts."

"There's one way to find out," Jessica said. "We have to talk to someone who knows Mayor Kugel better than anyone else. Wait here."

She opened the garage door and ran out.

When she came back, Professor Platt was with her.

"Ah, greetings! Are these future band members, perhaps?" he asked.

"Uh, Professor Platt," Jessica said. "You're friends with Mayor Kugel, right?"

"Well, yes," Professor Platt said with a laugh. "Even though he keeps complaining about my musicians. How did *you* think we sounded?"

"Flat," Max replied. "And loud."

"What does Mayor Kugel think about Crump's Playworld?" Jessica asked. "Just curious."

"Well, he gave a great speech at the Big Cleanup today," Professor Platt replied. "He was charming, well-spoken, inspiring —"

"But does he really think Crump's Playworld is good for the village of Rebus?" Quincy asked. "Really, truly, deep inside?"

Professor Platt took a deep breath and knelt down. "Between you and me, I know one thing that would make Mayor Kugel happy — if Crump's Playworld was gone and the Kugel Shopping Center was there instead."

Jessica looked at the others. It looked as if they had their man.

5

Danger at Dusk

"This Abracadabra Club meeting is now over!" Jessica said, tapping her magic wand on the table. It was the Monday after the Big Cleanup. It had been the worst meeting ever. They hadn't done one trick. Instead, they had just talked about Mayor Kugel and the Shazam Club — for almost an hour and a half.

Max, Quincy, Selena, and Jessica all

walked upstairs. Today, Jessica had to pick up Noah from the after-school program in the auditorium. It was already late, close to five o'clock. In the hallway, Jessica heard laughter and music from the gym.

They all peeked in. Kids were gathered around Bug and Andrew, trying on capes and top hats. "Everyone who joins today gets a genuine, gold Shazam Club Coin!" shouted Bug, holding up a small coin.

"Plus, you can see my worm collection!" Andrew called out. "A twenty-dollar value, free!"

"That's right, the Shazam Club — as seen on TV!" Bug went on. "The most famous magic club in Rebus. You've seen the rest — now join the best!"

"I can't watch this," Jessica said. "Let's get out of here."

They went around the corner to the auditorium. When Noah saw Jessica, he came running. "Jessie! Look! I'm a magician!"

Jessica's mouth dropped open. Noah was wearing a Shazam Club cape.

"Where did you get that?" she asked.

"It was free! I just had to write my name on a piece of paper Andrew gave me."

"You signed up for the Shazam Club?"

Noah's eyes started to water. "I did?"

Jessica sighed. Gently, she took the cape off her brother's shoulders. "Don't worry. I'll tell Andrew to erase your name. Let's go home."

Jessica headed outside. Max's dad was waiting for him in a car to take him to a dentist appointment. So Jessica walked home with Noah, Quincy, and Selena. As they passed the duck pond, Jessica made sure to turn in the direction of Crump's.

Crump's was closed on Mondays. In the

evening light, the glass building glowed orange. It looked like a postcard from the past. Jessica couldn't see the peeling paint and broken rides at all.

But she could see a person moving in the shadows.

She stopped short. "Someone's in there!"

"Where?" asked Quincy.

"By the merry-go-round! Look!" They all stood still and watched. The figure left the carousel building and headed for the rides in back. For a moment, the person stepped into the dying light.

Jessica could see a mass of curly brown hair. "Charlene?" she whispered.

"She told us she never goes near Crump's during the week," Quincy said.

"I knew it!" Selena exclaimed "She's trying to destroy the place. *She's* the one who broke everything. She has the keys. She hates Crump's. The lazy slob."

"Sshhh!" Jessica crouched near the Crump's parking lot fence. "Come on. And be quiet!"

"*Are you crazy?*" Selena said. "What if she sees us?"

"It's Charlene," said Quincy, "not King Kong."

Noah giggled. He was so excited, Jessica had to keep him from skipping ahead. Slowly, she tiptoed toward the entrance. Across it hung a CLOSED sign on a chain. Jessica ducked under it, followed by Quincy and Selena.

When Noah came through, he had a huge grin on his face. "I call first on the go-carts!"

He took off at a run.

"*No!*" Jessica tried to call him back, but

it was hard to yell and whisper at the same time. She raced after Noah, leaving Selena and Quincy behind. But Noah had disappeared around the carousel building.

The sun was setting behind their backs. The other side of the building was covered by a long, deep shadow. Jessica had to stop. Everything was gray and faded in the dim light. She wanted to call out to Noah and the others, but she knew she couldn't. She had to keep quiet. It was the only way to catch Charlene in the act.

Slowly, she moved forward. She held onto the carousel building wall. She passed by a hose, a metal lever with a sign over it that said DRAIN, and a glass ticket booth.

The other rides were just past the ticket booth. She tiptoed forward, her eyes straight ahead.

She wasn't looking at the booth when

someone jumped out. Someone with a mop of curly brown hair.

"AHHHH!" Jessica screamed.

"AHHHH!" screamed a deep voice.

Jessica knew it wasn't Charlene.

Charlene was not six feet tall.

6

A Hairy Mess

"Jessica, what happened?" asked Quincy, racing around the side of the building with Selena.

Jessica ran into him, panting. "A person . . . big . . . hair . . ."

"*Big hair?*" Selena said. "You saw Charlene?"

"It wasn't Charlene," Jessica said. "It

was huge — as tall as my dad! It — he — jumped out at me!"

"*Jessica, where are you?*"

It was Noah's voice, from behind them. He came running around the other side of the building. Jessica scooped him up in her arms. She didn't know whether to yell at him or kiss him.

"Ew, you're giving me cooties," Noah said.

Over Noah's shoulder, Jessica saw a car pull into the parking lot. The door opened and Grandpa Crump came out. "Hey, you! Who are you? Get off my property before I call the police!"

Jessica grabbed Noah's hand, and they all ran.

Two hours later, Max arrived at Jessica's house. Dinner was over, and Quincy and Se-

lena were already in the Frimmels' den. The TV was on, but no one was watching.

"I *knew* I should have walked home with you," Max said, taking off his coat. "I could have helped you. I know exactly how to scare away vampires."

"*It wasn't a vampire!*" Jessica said. "It was a person — disguised as Charlene!"

"Why would anyone want to be disguised as Charlene?" asked Selena.

Quincy opened his Clues book. "Mop-haired creature seen at Crump's . . ." he read aloud as he wrote.

On the TV, a commercial for the evening news started. The news anchors were looking very serious, and a photo of Grandpa Crump appeared beside them. "The latest in the Crump's Playworld saga — tonight, the owner, Mr. Elwood 'Grandpa' Crump, reported a daring break-in. Details at ten . . ."

"A *break-in*?" Jessica said.

The Frankie Fry's theme song now blared out of the TV. Happy families were walking into the restaurant, shaking hands with Mr. Spuds, the clown. "Hey-hey-hey, come to Frankie Fry's Franks 'n' Fries for our fabulous Friday Fries Fiesta!" Mr. Spuds said in a honking voice. "We're the fastest-growing, funnest, fast-food family frank-and-fries phenomenon in New England. And remember, look for a new Frankie Fry's Funland near *you*!"

"Turn that off," Selena said.

She reached for the remote, but Quincy stopped her. "Wait!" His eyes were fixed on the screen. "Look! What do you see?"

Max scratched his head. "French fries? Kids who can't act?"

"No!" Quincy began writing in his Clues Book. "You see someone who *does* have a motive to hurt Crump's. Someone opening new restaurants all over the place. Restaurants with *indoor* amusement parks."

"Frankie Fry's Funlands?" Selena asked.

"Quincy's right," Jessica said. "Frankie Fry's is growing fast. They need space. Crump's is huge. They could build the biggest Funland ever!"

"Jessica didn't see Charlene at all," Quincy added. "She saw a man — with a mop of curly hair. She saw Mr. Spuds."

"A clown, sneaking into Crump's at night?" Max said.

"No, the man who plays the clown!" Quincy replied. "I've seen him. His hair really looks like that. Think about it. Mr. Spuds was around during the Big Cleanup. But once the magic shows began, where was he? Where was Mr. Spuds when things started to go wrong?"

Max scratched his head. "I don't re-member seeing him. But I was too busy with our tricks."

Jessica thought about it. Mr. Spuds had been there for the Shazam Club's first trick, when they jumped onto the merry-go-round. But after that, she hadn't seen him until the very end. "The crowd was watching us and the Shazam Club," she said. "So were all the workers. Mr. Spuds could have easily snuck off into the shadows!"

"Then why was he there tonight?" Selena asked.

"To finish the job," Jessica replied. "But we must have scared him away. And if we hadn't, Grandpa Crump would have run right into him!"

Quincy slammed his book shut. "We have to tell Grandpa Crump before it's too late!"

7

Worm Catchers

Jessica looked at her digital watch. It said 7:13. She had never been to school this early. It was cold and gloomy, perfect weather for sleeping. But she knew that Mr. Beamish came to school at this hour. And she couldn't wait to tell him what the Abracadabra Club had discovered.

Selena was pacing the school lawn. Quincy was scribbling in his notepad. Max was napping on the grass, using his cape as a blanket.

"There he is!" Selena said nervously, pulling out her hairbrush. She nudged Max with her foot. "Wake up!"

Mr. Beamish's limo parked at the curb. It was the only car in history that wore a top hat — a huge metal one welded to the roof. Its radio antenna was a long magic wand, and over the trunk flowed a black canvas cape. On each side, a big sign said STANLEY BEAMISH/SEMI-FAMOUS WILD WEST MAGICIAN/ PARTIES FOR ALL AGES.

Jessica, Quincy, and Selena ran up to Mr. Beamish and told him what had happened. Mr. Beamish listened carefully as he climbed out of the car. Max stumbled sleepily behind them, dragging his magic wand.

"My dad tried calling Grandpa Crump last night," Jessica said. "But no one picked

up the phone. You have to help us. Do you know where we can find him?"

"Follow me." Mr. Beamish turned to walk up the street. "I know exactly where Grandpa Crump is. I know all the worm catchers in Rebus."

"Worm catchers?" asked Quincy.

"People who like to wake up before dawn," Mr. Beamish explained. "You know — the early bird catches the worm? Take me, for example. Each morning before school, I eat breakfast at a different coffee shop or diner. But Grandpa Crump likes the same place, day after day."

Jessica, Max, Quincy, and Selena followed Mr. Beamish. The Abracadabra Club parents all knew Mr. Beamish. They had signed permission slips allowing Mr. Beamish to take the members of the club off school grounds.

"Which place does Grandpa Crump like?" Jessica asked.

"The one that makes his favorite coffee in the world," Mr. Beamish replied. "Frankie Fry's Franks 'n' Fries."

"*What?*" said Jessica, Quincy, and Selena.

"*Whurrfsh?*" said Max, finally starting to wake up, but not quite.

"What are we going to tell him?" Selena was brushing her hair so fast, it was crackling. "That Mr. Spuds is out to destroy Crump's? He'll never believe it."

"The truth," said Mr. Beamish, "will never hurt you."

The closest Frankie Fry's was only two blocks from school. As Mr. Beamish held open the front door, he breathed in deeply. "Mm, smell those ham and eggs!"

Jessica swallowed hard. She looked

around for Mr. Spuds, but there was no sign of him. With a sigh, she walked inside. Frankie Fry's seemed a lot different in the mornings — quieter, with mostly older people and no kids.

Grandpa Crump was sitting with another man at a table by the window. Jessica ran toward him. "Excuse me, Grandpa Crump. I have something to tell you!"

The old man turned. His smile vanished. "You — you Abracadabra Club kids. You were the ones who broke into Playworld last night, weren't you?"

"Well — I — uh —" Jessica stared at the man sitting across from Grandpa Crump. He was wearing a knit cap pulled down to his ears. But something about his face was familiar.

"Yes, Elwood," the man said, pulling off his cap. "I saw them, too."

Jessica stepped back. The man's hair was curly and wild and brown. She thought she knew who he was. "Mr. Spuds?"

"Yup, even use my own hair," the man replied. "My real name's Frankie. Frankie Fry."

"You're Frankie Fry?" Quincy asked. "*The* owner of Frankie Fry's Franks 'n' Fries?"

"Every last one," said Frankie.

Max began reaching into his cape pockets. "Can I have your autograph?"

"*Mr. Fry* did it!" Selena cried out, pointing to Frankie. "We saw him!"

"He was sneaking around Crump's. In the dark." Jessica spoke so fast, she tripped over her words. "The outs were light — I mean, lights were out. I thought it was Charlene. With the hair. Then Noah ran inside. 'No,' I said. But he just kept running, and then I ran after him, but it was dark, and then I saw — him! *Frankie Fry is out to destroy Crump's!*"

Grandpa Crump took a deep breath. He took his napkin off his lap and folded it on the table.

Frankie Fry looked him straight in the eye. He slid his chair back.

"Frankie, is this true?" Grandpa Crump asked. "Were you sneaking around Crump's Playworld last night?"

"Why, yes, sir, I was," said Frankie Fry.

Jessica stuck close to Mr. Beamish's side. "Uh-oh," she said under her breath.

"What do we do now?" Selena whispered.

"C-c-call 911?" Quincy squeaked.

Then Grandpa Crump and Frankie Fry both burst out laughing.

"What's so funny?" Max asked.

"Mr. Fry was *meeting* me at Crump's Playworld that night," Grandpa Crump replied.

"Meeting you?" Jessica asked.

"He's a big fan of Crump's," Grandpa Crump explained. "He used to come when he was a kid. He heard about our troubles, and he wants to help."

Frankie Fry nodded. "We agreed that I would open up a Frankie Fry's Fun Fast Food stand — right in the Playworld Grill!"

"In return," Grandpa Crump said with a huge grin, "Mr. Fry has agreed to pay for fixing Crump's."

"The Ferris wheel?" asked Quincy.

"The boat rides?" said Selena.

"The coin-stamping machine?" added Max.

Frankie Fry nodded. "And maybe even

the old stage, where magic shows used to be performed."

"By magicians such as Stanley Beamish!" Mr. Beamish piped up.

"And the Abracadabra Club, I hope," Grandpa Crump added.

Jessica had to sit down. She felt so embarrassed. "I'm sorry," she said.

Grandpa Crump put his hand on her shoulder. "Don't be. In a way, you're the reason this all happened. You see, a little bird told me how concerned you were about Crump's. She knew how hard you worked at the Big Cleanup. And she was the one who gave me the idea to call Frankie Fry."

"Little bird?" Jessica asked. "Who was that?"

"My granddaughter," Grandpa Crump said with a smile, "dear, sweet Charlene."

8
Showdown

After meeting with Grandpa Crump, Mr. Beamish and the Abracadabra Club hurried back to school. They got there fifteen minutes before the morning bell.

Mr. Beamish rushed inside. But Jessica, Max, Selena, and Quincy walked slowly across the school lawn, deep in conversation.

"Okay, so if Mr. Spuds — er, Frankie Fry — didn't mess up the rides at the Big

Cleanup," Selena said, "and Charlene didn't do it, then that leaves one suspect."

"That would be Mayor Kugel," Quincy said with a nod. "But how can we *prove* he did it?"

Jessica shook her head. "I just can't believe this. He seems so nice."

Erica Landers, the snobbiest girl in the fourth grade, walked quickly past them. "Oh, hi," she said. "Sorry to hear the sad news about your club. 'Bye."

"Wait — *what* sad news?" asked Selena.

Erica looked over her shoulder. "That you broke up. Bug has been telling everybody. Too bad. Go Shazam Club!"

"Oh, *has* he?" said Jessica. She looked across the lawn. The Shazam Club was setting up a show. A crowd of kids had gathered to watch. Bug was waving the huge metal wand he'd used at the Big Cleanup. Andrew was on all fours, with a crystal ball on his back. "Step right up!" Bug cried out. "For the cost of one magic Shazam Club coin, the Globe of Truth will tell your fortune! One year of your future for each coin!"

"Let's put on our own show," Max said to Jessica, reaching into his cape and pulling out a long rope.

"Just a minute," Jessica said.

Noah came running across the lawn, holding out a shiny coin. "Look! I have one!"

Jessica neatly took it from him in her left hand. "Thank you very much. Now watch this." She walked through the crowd and stepped right up to Bug. "Tell what's in my future. And I'll tell you what's going to be history — the Shazam Club."

"Uh, I think it's time for school," Andrew said from below.

"Just stay there!" Bug said, then turned back to Jessica. "I'll tell your fortune, all right. But you have to give me the coin."

As Jessica handed it over, the coin shone in the morning light, making the words stand out bright and clear:

Jessica held it back, staring at the words. "Bug," she asked, "when did you make this?"

"Hand it over!" Bug said impatiently. "Or give up your place in line!"

Jessica's mind was racing. She had an idea, but she wasn't sure it would work. Taking the coin in her right hand, she made a fist.

Bug held out his hand. "Come on, give it to me."

Jessica opened her fist. The coin was gone.

"Cool!" shouted someone in the crowd. A few others started clapping.

"Where's the coin?" Bug asked.

"Oh, look!" Jessica cried out. "It's stuck to your magic wand."

Bug held up the metal wand. "What? Where?"

"Here!" Jessica took the wand. With her left hand, she pulled the coin right off the tip!

Now everyone was clapping. "And for my next trick, I shall make Bug disappear!"

Jessica said, grabbing Bug's wand and waving it.

Bug grinned. "Ha-ha! Didn't work!"

Jessica examined the wand carefully. "You're right. Hmm, that must mean this is not a real magic wand," she said. She looked around the crowd and saw Charlene Crump. "Charlene, does this wand look familiar to you?"

Charlene came forward. "Yeah. It's the pole that my grandpa uses to keep the power box closed on the Ferris wheel at Crump's Playworld."

"So, if it was taken," Jessica said, "then the box would open, and someone could make the Ferris wheel start turning?"

Andrew jumped to his feet. The Globe of Truth rolled to the grass. "Gotta go. My knees hurt."

"Not so fast," Jessica said, grabbing him

by the belt. "Andrew, did you take this pole from Crump's?"

Andrew's face was red. "I just wanted to see what was in the box, that's all!"

Jessica turned to the crowd, showing the coin. "Who can tell me where this comes from?"

"That's easy," said Erica Landers. "The Crump's coin-stamping machine."

"Which was broken for months, until the day of the Big Cleanup," said Jessica. "The only time this coin could have been made was *during* the cleanup. Which was when the machine started to spit coins!"

"It wasn't my fault!" Bruce Minsky blurted out. "I just kicked it a little."

Over the noise of the surprised crowd, Jessica called out, "Max, may I have your rope, please?"

Max pulled a rope from his backpack. It

was at least six feet long. He handed it to Jessica. "I was going to do a lasso trick," Jessica said, "but I changed my mind. Those are dangerous. Sometimes when you throw the lasso, it gets stuck. Like when Bug did his trick at the Big Cleanup. The rope got stuck around a big metal switch — the one that opens the drain for the boat ride! Making the water flood everywhere!"

"But — but I —" Bug sputtered.

"We don't want anything like that to happen again," Jessica said. "So I'll be safe and cut the rope into four smaller pieces." From her own backpack she pulled out a pair of scissors. She quickly sliced the rope until there were four sections. Each was about a foot and half long. With one short rope, she tied Max's wrists together. With the other, she tied Quincy's wrists together. But she made sure that Quincy's rope was looped through Max's, so they were attached to each other.

"The rule is: You may not untie the knots," Jessica announced. "Think you can get apart, Max and Quincy?"

The two boys began twisting their bodies around and twisting . . . and twisting. "Jessica, what are you doing to us?" Quincy asked.

"Hmm, this is hard even for the Abracadabra Club," Jessica said. "How about the Shazam Club?"

Andrew held out his arms. "No problem!"

"Easy for you to say," grumbled Bug.

"I propose a contest," Jessica said, tying the ends of the third rope around Andrew's wrists. "The Abracadabra Club against the Shazam Club. Whichever team gets apart first is the number one magic club in Rebus!"

She took the final small rope and looped it around Andrew's rope. Then she tied the ends around Bug's wrists. "May the best team win."

"One . . . two . . . three!" said Max and Quincy together. With a quick pull, they were separated — even though each boy's own wrists were still tied together!

"To school?" said Quincy.

"To school!" said Max.

"LONG LIVE THE ABRACADABRA CLUB!" shouted Jessica.

"YEEAAAA!" shouted the crowd.

RINNNNG! sounded the school bell.

Everyone walked into school, laughing and talking. Except for Bug and Andrew. They weren't laughing at all.

"Nice job, Jessica!" Selena said.

"You're a genius," Max agreed.

Quincy adjusted his glasses. "Yes. Well, I

was about to solve the mystery the same way . . ."

"Uh, Jessica?" asked Bug, dragging Andrew down the hallway. "Can we borrow your scissors?"

9

Franks, Fries, and a Big Surprise

"Welcome! Welcome!" shouted Grandpa Crump. "Free milkshakes today for all Abracadabra Club members!"

"Make mine chocolate!" Max said.

"This place looks great!" Noah cried out, gazing around the Crump's Playworld carousel building. Everything was clean, shiny, and in working order.

84

"And wait till you see Filbert," Grandpa Crump said. "He got a new coat of paint."

"Silly, horses don't wear coats," Noah said. "They wear saddles!"

Mr. Beamish came rushing in the door of the new Playworld Grill. "Big crowd today," he said.

"Should be," said Grandpa Crump, bringing a tray of drinks to the table. "Crump's Playworld passed inspection this morning with flying colors!"

"YYYES!" shouted Jessica.

"Congratulations!" said Mr. Beamish.

Selena stood, holding her Shirley Temple. "Let's clink glasses to celebrate!"

"Grandpa Crump, do you still have my favorite drink?" Quincy asked.

Grandpa Crump pulled out a bottle of prune juice from the refrigerator case. "I know my customers!"

"Why are you looking at me like that?" Quincy said to Selena and Jessica. "I just like the taste."

Jessica never could understand that about Quincy. But it didn't matter. Today was the grand reopening of Crump's Playworld. Three weeks had passed since the Big Cleanup. The Ferris wheel was spinning again. The boat ride had a new, computerized drain control. The coin-stamping machine had been fixed. The Playground Grill had a brand-new Frankie Fry's Fun Fast Food counter.

Best of all, Crump's was back in business — inspected and all!

Jessica, Max, Quincy, Selena, and Noah clinked glasses. "Drink fast," Jessica said. "Our show starts in five minutes."

Max drank his soda and rushed over to the Frankie Fry's counter. Today it was being run by Frankie Fry himself — dressed as Mr. Spuds.

"One order of Frankie's Fabulous Fries," Max announced. Then he lowered his voice to a whisper. "I know who you really are."

Mr. Spuds served Max his order. Then he beeped his french-fry nose. A flower on his jacket squirted water in Max's face.

Mr. Beamish laughed. "Clowns are like magicians. They never really grow up!"

Max returned to the table, wiping water from his face. "I always fall for that trick."

Quincy was looking in his Mystery Log, puzzled. "Jessica, I still can't figure out exactly how you solved the mystery."

"Bug's coins gave him away," Jessica said. "I knew he had a lot of them. That meant *someone* was at the coin-stamping machine, making those coins, when it broke.

Once I realized that, the other clues started making sense. Like the lasso, which got caught around the drain lever. And the magic wand — or, I should say, the Ferris wheel pole."

"I should have known," Selena said. "I hung our Abracadabra Club banner on that pole when it was still on the power box!"

"Why didn't the Shazam Club just tell the truth?" Quincy asked.

"They were afraid," Selena replied. "They thought they would be punished."

"Well, they were right," Mr. Beamish said. "Mr. McElroy won't let them meet in school anymore."

"And they all have to write essays on 'What Honesty Means to Me,'" Quincy added.

Jessica quickly slurped down her shake. "Okay, enough talk. Are we ready?"

"READY!" said Quincy, Max, and Selena.

They all stood up and walked out of the Playground Grill toward a new performance space. There, a big crowd was waiting.

Charlene Crump turned to the crowd. "Thank you for coming to opening day of the new, improved Crump's Playworld, everybody!" she said into a microphone. "And now, what you've all been waiting for — the Abracadabra Club!"

A huge cheer went up. Charlene smiled.

"Charlene, I can't believe how much you changed," Jessica whispered, tightening the bow of her magic cape.

"I thought you hated Crump's," Max said.

Charlene shrugged. "I still hate it. Sort of. Now that things are better here, Grandpa can afford to hire a real helper. That means I won't have to help out on weekends anymore. This is my last day."

Jessica, Quincy, Max, and Selena stepped forward and took a bow. Jessica looked over the faces in the crowd.

There, in the front row, sat Bug and Andrew.

Taking notes.

The Abracadabra Files by Quincy
Magic Trick #22
The Old Elbow Rub

Ingredients:
One coin
One elbow

How Jessica Did It:

1. When Bug gave Jessica his quarter, she took it in her right hand. Then she began rubbing the quarter against her left forearm — the part above the elbow. Important Part of the Trick #1: She rubbed it with her palm facing inward, so no one could see the coin (figure a).

2. Then the quarter dropped to the floor (figure b). Everyone thought she had made a mistake. But she hadn't. She picked up the quarter, with her *left* hand (figure c). Important Part of the Trick #2: She kept talking as she appeared to pass the coin to her right hand (figure d). The crowd was paying attention to what she was saying, so they weren't

seeing what *really* happened — Jessica had actually *kept* the quarter in her left hand!

3. As she rubbed the "quarter" into her elbow again with her palm facing toward her, the same as before (figure e), she was really rubbing . . . nothing (figure f)!

4. Meanwhile, her left arm was crooked upward — so she could simply drop the quarter down the front of her shirt.

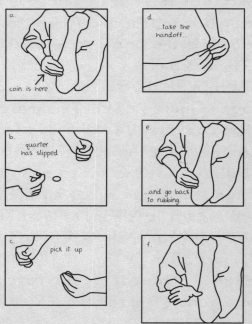

The Abracadabra Files by Quincy
Magic Trick #23
A Knotty Problem!

Ingredients:
One rope, about four or five feet long
One pair of scissors

How Jessica Did It:

1. She took the end of the rope and tied a square knot in the middle, making a loop like the one I drew at the right. (figures a-d).
2. Then, with the scissors, she cut the loop (figures e-f). This makes a knot that can easily be slipped off.
3. She held out the rope from both ends, to show that the knot was in the middle. Then she began wrapping the rope around her left hand (figure g). With her right hand, she pulled off the knot (figure h).
4. When she unwrapped the rope, the knot was gone (figure i)!

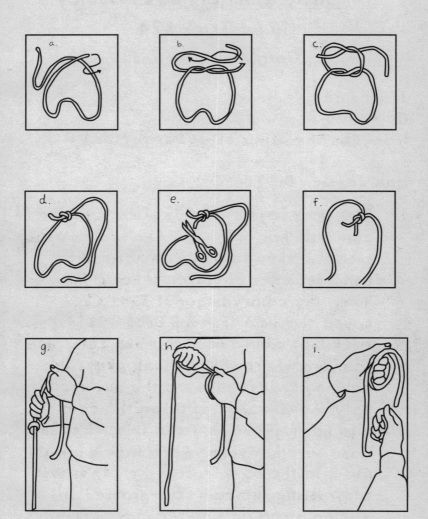

The Abracadabra Files by Quincy
Magic Trick #24
Coin on the Wand

Ingredients:
Coin
Wand (or any other object or person)

How Jessica Did It:

1. The trick began when Jessica took the coin with her left hand. She looked at it closely, then took it with her right hand. But when she opened her right hand, the coin was gone! That's because she did a "French Drop." It is a trick that can be used to make coins appear anywhere. She actually kept the coin in her left hand, so the audience only *thought* she had taken the coin into her right hand. To do this, first she made sure her palms were facing inward (to hide the coin from sight). Instead of grabbing the coin, she grabbed air. The coin *remained in the cupped fingers* of her left hand. But since her palm was facing in, no one noticed.

96

2. She opened her right palm — no coin! Then she reached for the top of the wand *with her left hand, which had the coin*. It looked like she was taking the coin off the wand!

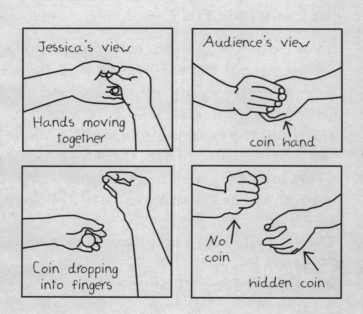

The Abracadabra Files by Quincy
Magic Trick #25
All Tied Up

Ingredients:
Two lengths of rope, about 1½ feet long each

How Max and I Did It:

1. Good acting was important (and HOURS of practice)! We only pretended that we were struggling. Honestly, we could have won an Oscar! While we were grunting and twisting around, I pushed the center of my rope through Max's wrist loop (figures a-b). It was *very* important for Max to stay still — and he did.
2. Then I pulled my rope over Max's hand (figures c-d).
3. We yanked free (figure e)!

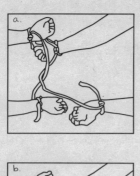

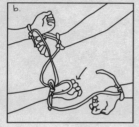

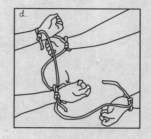

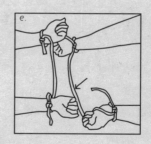

About the Author

Peter Lerangis is the author of many different kinds of books for many ages, including *Watchers*, an award-winning science-fiction/mystery series; *Antarctica*, a two-book exploration adventure; and several hilarious novels for young readers, including *Spring Fever!*, *Spring Break*, *It Came from the Cafeteria*, and *Attack of the Killer Potatoes*. His movie adaptations include *The Sixth Sense*. He lives in New York City with his wife, Tina deVaron, and their two sons, Nick and Joe.

Look for the next book in the

series,
coming soon.

Mr. Beamish was the best teacher Jessica Frimmel had ever had. He did magic tricks in class. He drove a car with a giant top hat on its roof. He moved fast and said funny things. He liked to say he was going, going, going — going bald, going gray, going full-steam ahead.

One Tuesday, his class thought he was going crazy. That was the day he opened his mail, jumped up from his desk, and shouted, "Yahoo — we did it!"

"We *didn't!*" said Selena Cruz, who was often contrary.

"We did it," declared Jessica, who was very proud.

"We did what?" asked Andrew Flingus, who was always confused.

Mr. Beamish held up a sheet of paper. On top, in huge letters, it said,

Olde Brattle Village
Hiftorical Conteft
Firft Place:
Rebuf Elementary School
the claffef of Mr. Beamifh
& Mr. Norbert
"Legendf and Magickal Artf
of Olde Brattle Village"

Andrew scratched his head. "Hiftory conteft?"

"It's *history contest*," explained Quincy. "In Colonial America, the letter *S* sometimes looked like the letter *F*."

This was big news. The biggest news in Rebus Elementary School.

Brattle Village was sometimes called the "Old Ghost Town of Massachusetts." In colonial times, it had been a short horse ride away from Rebus. But in 1798, a fire burned the village to the ground. Over the years, it had been nearly forgotten — until students from Rebus College found original plans and drawings. They began digging up old pots and pans, stone fences, and basements. Working with historians and builders, they organized a restoration of the whole village.

Now it was ready to open. It would have dirt roads and old-fashioned houses and shops. No cars or modern things would be allowed. Actors were going to play real people from the past. Kids would play Colonial American children — but only kids who won the class contest.

Mr. Beamish's and Mr. Norbert's classes had worked together collecting maps and drawings, and researching history and legends. They sent in their project weeks ago.

Mr. Beamish began reading aloud: "'We, the founders of Old Brattle Village, congratulate the winners of our conteft — er, contest — for their project, *Legends and Magickal Arts of Old Brattle Village*. It will become part of our new book, *A History of Old Brattle Village*. Each of you will receive one free copy. We hereby invite you to be 'Village Children' in our opening weekend, two weeks from Saturday. We will train you to act like colonial children from Old Brattle Village. You will wear costumes from the seventeen hundreds. We hope that you will perform magic tricks.'"

"*YIPPEE!*" said Jessica.

The whole class stood and cheered.